# In the Jerusalem Forest

*To Chen-Ayala, my beloved daughter*
*from Ima, Devora. —D.B.*

*To my daughter Daria, who sees every puddle as a magical pond,*
*from Ima, Noa. —N.K.*

Photo credit: Jewish Chronicle/Heritage Images/Getty Images p.32.
© 2019 by Devora Busheri
Illustrations copyright © 2019 Noa Kelner

Originally published in Hebrew by Mizrahi Publishing

KAR-BEN PUBLISHING, INC.
A division of Lerner Publishing Group, Inc.
241 First Avenue North
Minneapolis, MN 55401 USA
1-800-4-KARBEN

Website address: www.karben.com

Main body text set in Mikado Regular 18/30.
Typeface provided by HDV Fonts.

**Library of Congress Cataloging-in-Publication Data**

Names: Busheri, Devora, 1967–author. | Rosenak-Kelner, Noa, illustrator.
Title: In the Jerusalem forest / by Devora Busheri ; illustrated by Noa Kelner.
Description: Minneapolis : Kar-Ben Publishing, [2019] | Series: Israel | Series:
   Kar-Ben favorites | Summary: A girl and her mother walk in a forest, growing in
   their appreciation of nature and of each other, especially as they gaze into a still
   pond. Includes note about Haim Nachman Bialik, on whose poem, "The Pond,"
   the story is based.
Identifiers: LCCN 2018033351| ISBN 9781541534728 (lb : alk. paper) |
   ISBN 9781541534735 (pb : alk. paper)
Subjects: | CYAC: Mother and child—Fiction. | Nature—Fiction. | Forests and
   forestry—Fiction. | Jerusalem—Fiction.
Classification: LCC PZ7.1.B8877 In 2019 | DDC [E]—dc23

LC record available at https://lccn.loc.gov/2018033351

PJ Library Edition ISBN 978-1-72841-286-3

Manufactured in China
1-48538-49040-9/26/2019

042033.8K1/B1492/A3

# In the Jerusalem Forest

**Devora Busheri**

Illustrations by **Noa Kelner**

KAR-BEN
PUBLISHING

לְבַדָּהּ תַּחֲלֹם לָהּ חֲלוֹם עוֹלָם הָפוּךְ

וְתִדְגֶּה לָהּ בַּחֲשַׁאי אֶת־דְּגֵי זְהָבָהּ -

וְאֵין יוֹדֵעַ מַה־בִּלְבָבָהּ.

– חַיִּים נַחְמָן בְּיַאלִיק, "הַבְּרֵכָה"

Alone, she dreams of an upside-down world,

secretly catching her fish of gold.

And no one can know what her heart beholds.

—From Hayim Nahman Bialik's "The Pond"

Winter has gone.

Spring has come.

Everything blossoms and blooms
in the sun.

Hand in hand, under the blue sky,
in the Jerusalem forest walk Ima and I.

In the shade
I see a small pond.
"Ima, wait!" I say. "Look!"

"There in the water: the sky!"
And at my feet
are cypress and pine.
The forest is upside-down.

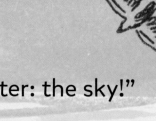

Ima and I see our
reflections in the pond.
We look the same,
like two drops of rain.

Now the wind blows.
**Whoosh!**
A leaf falls from above,
floats down, and decorates my hair.

But something has changed,
a ripple in the water . . .

Where did the upside-down forest go?

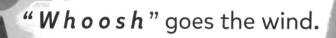

"**Whoosh**" goes the wind.

"Ima, I want to hug you."

The clouds disappear.
Everything blossoms and blooms
in the sun.
The world is wonderful.

In the pond
we looked exactly the same,
like two drops of rain.
Between the water and the sky,
Ima and I.

# Author's Note

Hayim Nahman Bialik was born in 1873 in the Zhitomir district, in the days of the Russian Empire. From his first poem, "To the Bird," and throughout his life, his poetry was acclaimed by his people. While he initially wrote in Yiddish, he later wrote in Hebrew.

Bialik wrote poetry that captured the minds and hearts of his fellow Jews. He became known as the "poet of the Jewish renaissance," and ultimately, as Israel's national poet.

Bialik was only seven when his father died, and he was raised by his Orthodox grandfather. He received a Jewish religious education, but he was also very interested in exploring European literature.

He became attracted to the Jewish Enlightenment movement (Haskala), and slowly drifted away from yeshiva life. Later on he was influenced by Ahad Ha'am, a Hebrew essayist and Zionist thinker.

In 1924, Bialik moved to Israel, devoting himself to cultural activities and public affairs. He died in 1934. His house at 22 Bialik Street in Tel Aviv is now a museum.

Bialik's poem "The Pond," on which this picture book is based, is a beautiful exploration of the relationship between Torah and reality, asking the question:

## *"Which is the reflection of which?"*

## About Author

**Devora Busheri** is a children's book writer, editor and translator. She has authored six books and edited many others for various publication houses in Israel. Devora lives in Jerusalem with her husband and their four children.

## About Illustrator

**Noa Kelner** graduated from the Bezalel Academy of Art & Design. Her illustrations have appeared in books, newspapers, and magazines, and loves to give stories color and form. She is the co-founder and artistic director of the annual "Outline–Illustration and Words" festival in Jerusalem and also teaches illustration. She lives in Jerusalem with her husband and two children.